Ronnie and Aunt Martha took turns keeping a lookout toward the mainland through the keeper's glass. But no little boat marred the green surface of the open sea. At suppertime Aunt Martha found Ronnie crouched in the deep windowseat of one of the tower's upper windows, the glass still clutched in his hands.

"It's been a disappointing day, Ronnie, I know," she said gently. "But come now, dear, and help me with the light."

He didn't answer, and she went on, "What's one more night? We'll light our lantern and then we'll have our tea. There's a hot fish chowder simmering on the stove this minute."

Ronnie turned a grim little face towards her. "It isn't that it's just one more night," he said. "But he promised. . . ."

"I know he promised, Ronnie. But something may have happened. We can't know. Let's not be too hard on him. Like as not he'll be here tomorrow. Come now. Whatever happens, our lamp must burn. . . ."

"Will be appreciated by thoughtful readers who are receptive to the poetic sense of the sea."   —*New York Times*

The Light
at Tern Rock

BY JULIA L. SAUER

Illustrated by Georges Schreiber

PUFFIN BOOKS

PUFFIN BOOKS

Published by the Penguin Group

Penguin Books USA Inc., 375 Hudson Street, New York, New York 10014, U.S.A.

Penguin Books Ltd, 27 Wrights Lane, London W8 5TZ, England

Penguin Books Australia Ltd, Ringwood, Victoria, Australia

Penguin Books Canada Ltd, 10 Alcorn Avenue, Toronto, Ontario, Canada M4V 3B2

Penguin Books (N.Z.) Ltd, 182–190 Wairau Road, Auckland 10, New Zealand

Penguin Books Ltd, Registered Offices: Harmondsworth, Middlesex, England

First published in the United States of America by The Viking Press, 1951
Published in Puffin Books, 1994

40

LIBRARY OF CONGRESS CATALOGING-IN-PUBLICATION DATA
Sauer, Julia L. (Julia Lina)
[Light at Christmas]
The light at Tern Rock/Julia L. Sauer; illustrated by Georges Schreiber.
p.   cm.—(Puffin Newbery library)
"Originally published in The horn book under the title 'The light
at Christmas' "—T.p. verso.
"A Newbery honor book"—P. [4] of cover.
"Ages 8–12"—P. [4] of cover.
Summary: Ronnie and his aunt take care of the lighthouse while the
keeper is on vacation, and when he does not return as expected, they
discover that Tern Rock is a perfect place to spend Christmas.
ISBN 0-14-036857-4
[1. Lighthouses—Fiction. 2. Christmas—Fiction.] I. Schreiber,
Georges, ill. II. Title.
PZ7.S25Li   1994   [Fic]—dc20   93-36242   CIP   AC
Originally published in *The Horn Book* under the title "The Light at Christmas."

Printed in the United States of America

To

Lois

in happy remembrance

of many a Christmas Eve

Contents

The Light at Tern Rock

Ashore

"WHY, Mrs. Morse, what boy *wouldn't* relish a holiday in a lighthouse? Especially a Light like Tern Rock—way out to sea and all?" The keeper of Tern Rock Lighthouse tossed his cap on the table and drummed impatiently on the arms of his chair.

Martha Morse answered him quietly. "I don't doubt that Ronnie would enjoy it, Mr. Flagg. But I don't like the idea of taking him out of school for two weeks. He's doing well this fall, and children shouldn't be uprooted just to suit the convenience of their elders."

"School!" Byron Flagg's shrug showed how little he thought of school, and Mrs. Morse smiled.

"You see," she said, "it isn't as if Ronnie were my own child. I think I feel even more responsible for him because he's a nephew. Maybe," she continued, "you could find someone else."

The keeper's face screwed up with disappointment. "It's like I told you, Mrs. Morse." He tried hard to sound persuasive. "The Superintendent said if I could find me a substitute that knows the Light, I could take an extra shore leave and pay 'em myself. I've gone over everybody in my mind that was ever stationed out there. You're the only one I can reach. You know that Light and what it's like out there. You can spell me for a fortnight same as if you was a man. And with the boy to keep you company, the time'll pass mighty fast. Provisions and supplies are all aboard. Everything's battened down, ready for winter. It'll be an easy fortnight for you."

He paused and looked across at her with his shrewd old eyes. When he spoke again, his voice was very casual.

"How long was it you lived on the Rock?" he asked.

"Fourteen years," Mrs. Morse told him. "My husband was keeper there for fourteen years."

She rose from her chair and walked over to the window. She stood looking out at the cold, gray-green November afternoon, at the little path that wound between the spruces to the road. Hers was the last house on the edge of the village and she had chosen it purposely. She had lived fourteen years without neighbors, and she was wise enough to know that the threads of village life must be taken up again gradually. Only so could she bear to part with the beauty and isolation of Tern Rock.

The fresh birch logs crackled in the shining range and the smooth neat kitchen grew darker. The keeper gave her plenty of time. He pursed his lips into a tight line to hide the little grin that was edging its way in. Then he spoke very softly but as if there had been no interruption.

"Fourteen years, now! I've only been out there five but I've learned one thing already. You can't live on Tern Rock without its doing something to you. And down inside, right this minute"—his voice fell to a whisper—"right this minute, you're longing to go back.

You're wishing you could watch the spray flung back on the ledge. You're wishing you could stand out there against the sea wall and listen and listen — and listen."

Mrs. Morse turned toward him quickly, and he laughed out loud at the change in her face. "I'm right, ain't I? I can tell you want to go. Oh, come now, and give an old man a good long leave. Let the boy's teacher set him some sums, and you hear his spelling and his reading. He'll be all the wiser for a stay on the old Rock."

Mrs. Morse smiled suddenly, and the keeper knew he had won.

"You're right, Mr. Flagg," she said. "But what business has a man to know so well how a woman feels about places where she's been happy? You've got wisdom, Mr. Flagg. Maybe it's the wisdom of the serpent because you've certainly tempted me against my better judgment. I do believe I'm homesick for the Rock — even if it *is* the lonesomest place in the world. I'd like to accommodate you, but I've got to admit that if I go it's for selfish reasons."

She hesitated and then spoke more sharply. "But how do you know you'll be able to get us off when your leave's up? You know, well as I do, that weeks and weeks can go by and not a chance of landing on the Rock. You say you'll come for us by December fifteenth. But how can you be sure?"

"Oh, there won't be nothing worse than a three-day blow — not in December. That wouldn't hold you up long."

The woodshed door banged suddenly and there was a sound of running feet.

"Aunt Marthy! Aunt Marthy! Guess what!" The kitchen door flew open and Ronnie burst in. "We began to practice Christmas carols today! Oh —" He stopped when he saw that his aunt had a guest.

Martha Morse smiled at him. "Shut the door tight, Ronnie. There's a cold wind. We've got company. Mr. Flagg, this is my nephew Ronnie, son of my husband's brother. Mr. Flagg is keeper of Tern Rock Lighthouse, Ronnie — where your Uncle Irvin and I used to be."

"Howdy, Ronnie. How'd you like to spend a fortnight on the Rock yourself? Wouldn't that be something, now, to tell the fellows about?"

The face of the sturdy small boy lit up and he gave

a long whistle. "I'd sure like to see Tern Rock Light. But—" He stopped and looked at his aunt.

"But what, Ronnie?" she asked. "Go on."

"Would we be home for Christmas?" Ronnie asked bluntly.

"For Christmas? Holy mackerel—yes! And long before," the keeper answered for her. "I'm only asking your aunt to go out till the fifteenth. I'll be back by then sure! Yessir! Not a day later than the fifteenth. I just want to make a little visit to a niece and her family over beyond St. John. And I can't do it on my five-day leave. You'd like to go, wouldn't you, boy?"

"I'd rather go some other time—not so close to Christmas," Ronnie said honestly. "But I would like to go. *Are* we going, Aunt Marthy?"

"I reckon so, Ronnie. And I know you'll enjoy it."

"Great! That's settled then, ma'am." The keeper had gained his point and he wanted to be on his way before she could change her mind. "I'll see that the Superintendent knows. You and the boy'll go out on Thursday and take over from my relief, Wilbert Denton. He's out there now. And I'll see that you get word when to be down to the shore.

"Yes, and I'll arrange for somebody to give you a hand with your luggage. You'll want all your warm duds. And thank you, Mrs. Morse, thank you."

"Mr. Flagg, just a minute!" Martha Morse's quiet gray eyes held the keeper's reluctant ones, and she spoke firmly. "You give me your word you'll come for us on the fifteenth?"

"Sure, Mrs. Morse — on the fifteenth, without fail. 'Course," he added casually, "if there's a blow, it'll be a day or two later. But I'll be out for you. And, boy" — he turned to Ronnie — "you'll think Tern Rock is a little piece of Heaven!"

Aboard the Rock

Ronnie, swathed in borrowed oilskins three sizes too big for him, sat crouched in the stern of the relief boat that was taking them out to the Rock. When he sighted it first on the horizon, shaped like a low-lying ship, he turned to call to his aunt. But Martha Morse had sighted it too. Her face was gayer and younger than Ronnie had ever seen it. She nodded and smiled and called something to him that was lost in the wind, but he knew that she was happy and as excited as he.

At the little landing on the southwest side of Tern Rock they were put ashore hurriedly. The wind was shifting, and the men were eager to put back. The luggage was carried in, Wilbert Denton gave them a few last instructions, turned over the keys to the stores, and stepped aboard the boat. Ten minutes later it was a mere speck rising and falling in the green troughs.

A middle-aged woman and an eleven-year-old boy were alone on Tern Rock. In their hands rested the safety of every ship plying the sea lanes within sight of its flashing light.

Ronnie stood close to the base of the tower and looked around him. He knew that Tern Rock was two hundred feet long, but it looked as small as a platter in the great expanse of heaving water that seemed above them on all sides — ready to break and wash over them. He leaned back and looked up toward the lantern where terns and gulls and gannets circled and wheeled, soared and dipped, in a rhythmic pattern. The birds' mewing cries, the waves' hollow gulps pulling in and out of the rock crevices, the hiss of spray — these were the sounds of Tern Rock. In storms they would rise and roar in crescendo, they would hush to muted murmurs

in still weather, but they would be the ever-present music. Dizzily he clutched the tower wall for support as a sudden wave of responsibility seemed to wash over him. He caught his breath sharply and turned to his aunt, his sudden doubt of their ability showing in his startled eyes.

But Martha Morse understood. She smiled confidently and gave him an encouraging little shake. "I know, Ronnie," she said. "I always used to feel like that, too, whenever I came aboard of the Rock. We mortals seem just too pindling to be trusted with this God-made pile of rock and this man-made pile of masonry. But remember this. If you and I weren't here, and this Light was left alone, this Rock and these ledges would be nothing but a danger and a menace. We're needed. And we can do what's expected of us. Now come, let's go inside. We'll get unpacked and settled. We'll make our bunks up first. Then we'll plan supper. And then we'll explore."

Everything about the lighthouse was a delight to Ronnie. The main room, which was kitchen and living room combined, seemed the warmest, friendliest room he had ever seen. Its smooth gray walls reflected every dancing shadow, and its compactness, its neatness, was as perfect as that of any ship. The built-in cupboards gave it a spacious air for all its smallness. The chairs were comfortable, or would be for longer legs, the table satin-smooth and sturdy. There were books in a wall bookcase, and games carved from wood. There was a built-in dresser with cheerful, heavy dishes. It was a room where one could feel, and be, a man, and the blossoming rose geraniums and heliotrope on a little window stand only made him feel more manly, somehow, in contrast to their frailty. On another level were two small bunk rooms with built-in, curtained bunks high above the floor, the space beneath filled with generous drawers in which to stow one's gear. Ronnie was proud when Aunt Martha took for granted that he would want to have a whole bunk room to himself.

After three days, life on Tern Rock settled into an even pattern. Every daylight hour was filled with busyness; every hour of dark with quiet pastimes. Aunt Martha laid out a schedule for them both. She herself turned out the light at daybreak. Then, while it cooled, there was breakfast for her to get and the morning

housework for her to do, and a run outdoors for Ronnie, or a bit of fishing. Both of them were needed to clean the lantern, to polish the great lens, to wind the clockwork that drove its revolving mechanism, to pump the oil up to the lamp chamber, and to do all the other routine tasks. There was time before their dinner for an hour of study too, and there were two hours of schoolwork in the afternoon, with Aunt Martha playing teacher. Together, at dusk, they climbed the iron stairs to light the lamp. And together they always watched it for a moment as its regular rhythmic flash pierced the growing dark — one, one two, one; one, one two, one. When they were sure that all was going properly, they climbed down the spiral stairs to the snug common room. Then supper, games and books, and bed.

Martha Morse watched Ronnie with some surprise. She had her memories here to live on, but it was strange, she thought, for such an active boy, one who was the center of his gang at school, to fit so easily into the monotony of their quiet life. But there he was before her eyes, happy and busy, poking his nose into every corner like a healthy puppy.

"It would be fun to have a dog, Aunt Marthy," he

said one day. "Why do you suppose Mr. Flagg doesn't keep a dog?"

"You can't keep a dog out here," she told him. "They say it's been tried and they go mad, but I don't know if it's true."

"Really mad?" Ronnie was aghast.

"Well, they don't develop rabies, I don't suppose, but they go out of their minds all the same unless you take them ashore."

Another day Ronnie came in panting and out of breath. "I've hunted and hunted over every inch of this Rock—and I can't find one single blade of grass. It seems funny that a little bit doesn't grow here by accident!"

"The Rock's had its share of accidents—of another kind. There've been wrecks, horrible wrecks, on this ledge. I've seen three myself, and many's the good ship that piled on these rocks in the old days before the Light was built. Lighthouses, Ronnie, are like a helping hand reaching out from Heaven itself. And the tending of them is good work—*good*," his aunt told him.

Doldrums

DECEMBER fifteenth was upon them before they had time to be weary of their bargain. It dawned clear and fine.

"The keeper'll be sure to come today. The sea's as smooth as anything," Ronnie said at breakfast. "It's been fun, but I'll be glad to get home."

"Yes, thank goodness, it's a fine day," Aunt Martha agreed. "We'll pack our belongings early — the minute we get the lantern cleaned and our chores done. We must leave everything as neat as a ship's cabin. Like as not the boat won't want to wait five minutes, so we'd best be ready."

The fine clear day wore on. Lessons were put aside, and Ronnie and Aunt Martha took turns keeping a lookout toward the

mainland through the keeper's glass. But no little boat marred the green surface of the open sea. At suppertime Aunt Martha found Ronnie crouched in the deep windowseat of one of the tower's upper windows, the glass still clutched in his tired hands.

"It's been a disappointing day, Ronnie, I know," she said gently. "But come now, dear, and help me with the light."

He didn't answer, and she went on, "What's one more night? We'll light our lantern and then we'll have our tea. There's a hot fish chowder simmering on the stove this minute."

Ronnie turned a grim little face toward her. "It isn't that it's just one more night," he said. "But he *promised*, Aunt Marthy. I heard him my own self. 'Not a day later than the fifteenth,' he said. I heard him say it."

"I know he promised, Ronnie. But something may have happened. We can't know. Let's not be too hard on him. Like as not he'll be here tomorrow. Come now. Whatever happens, our lamp must burn. And I need your help. No woman can manage it alone."

Ronnie jumped down to the steps and plodded wearily up toward the lamp room without another word.

The next day was the same, and the next; the eighteenth, the nineteenth, the twentieth, the twenty-first and the twenty-second of December came and went, and still no boat from Twin Islands or the mainland. Nothing, beyond the fringe of flying spray as wave met rock, but the vast expanse of gray-green water.

Ronnie said very little. He did his share of the work with a hard, unsmiling face. Wise Martha Morse knew that something deeper than disappointment was gnawing at him. His sense of justice had been outraged; Byron Flagg hadn't played fair. But wisely, too, she waited for him to speak. It came one night as they were doing up their dishes after tea.

Ronnie flung down his towel and burst out, "Aunt Marthy, isn't a broken promise the wickedest thing on earth?"

Martha Morse took her hands out of the water and gave the question her full attention. "I don't believe so," she said gravely at last. "It seems to me I can think of wickeder things. I guess cruelty — hurting anything little or defenseless — is my idea of the worst kind of wickedness. Still, I can remember when I'd have agreed with you," she added honestly. "But you get used to broken promises, Ronnie. Broken promises, along with good intentions that have gone wrong, just litter the highway all through your life. They're nothing to bother about much unless they're your own. But they're *mean*, Ronnie. A man who breaks a promise has a weak place in his net. Sometimes he'll get by with it, but sometime he'll lose the catch of a lifetime. But we've got to remember one thing before we dare to judge Byron Flagg or anyone else — we've got to know why he broke his promise. Maybe he had a good reason."

Ronnie showed no interest in Byron Flagg's reason, but he said fiercely as he picked up his towel again, "I'll never break a promise as long as I live!"

Martha Morse made no comment, but she thought to herself, "If he can live up to that, he'll be in debt to Byron Flagg."

When they finished breakfast on the morning of the twenty-third, Martha Morse put her elbows firmly on the table, rested her chin in her two hands, and looked across at Ronnie. Her face was serene and her keen gray eyes were almost smiling. Almost, Ronnie thought, as if she knew a secret.

"Ronnie," she began, "we may as well face the facts. Byron Flagg's not coming before Christmas. Now I've never spent Christmas in my life in any place that I haven't scrubbed till it shone, and I'm not going to begin now. You and I are going to start right in. By night this whole lighthouse has got to shine like the lamp itself."

"Oh, Aunt Marthy," Ronnie protested, "it's clean as a whistle! There's not a speck of dust anywhere."

His aunt laughed at him. "I know it," she said. "But we'll give it an extra loving polish anyhow—just because it's Christmas."

"A *loving* polish," Ronnie grumbled.

"Ronnie," Mrs. Morse said gently, "for hundreds and hundreds of years men have believed that on Christmas Eve the Christ Child goes visiting. He goes into all kinds of homes. None is too poor, too distant. That's why we make our houses as lovely as we can. We must be ready."

"But we can't trim it up one tiny bit. We haven't a single thing to make it look Christmasy."

"We can give it the beauty of perfect cleanliness," she said. "And tomorrow we'll bake!"

"Bake what?" Ronnie demanded.

"I don't know yet, but I'll ransack the keeper's stores and see what I can find. I'll fashion some kind of pudding! You'll see! And no woman can call herself a cook who can't work a miracle with spices and molasses. But today, remember, we scrub! I want you to begin on the storage locker on the second landing. There's nothing heavy there—just light cases. You can move them easily and set them back when you've finished."

Her energy was contagious, and Ronnie melted a little.

"All right, Aunt Marthy," he said more good-naturedly, "if you say shine, we'll shine. But it won't hurry that mean old Flagg along."

They hurried through the breakfast work and did the lamp with scrupulous care before Ronnie started on his storage locker.

Fifteen minutes later Mrs. Morse was startled by a shout from above.

"Aunt Marthy, come *quick!* See what I've found!"

"What on earth is it? Don't tell me you've found Byron Flagg himself packed in the locker!" She laughed as she flew up the stairs.

Ronnie was kneeling beside a seaman's chest. "Look!

It's got my name on it!" he said excitedly. "How can there be a box here for me? And it says 'Christmas greetings' on it too. That's funny."

He looked up at his aunt. At the sight of her face, full of concern, the answer came to him too. The laughter died out of his face and he put his head down on the chest and shook with dry sobs. But in a moment he was on his feet, his face white with anger.

"He planned this whole thing, Aunt Marthy, didn't he? He knew all along he was going to leave us here. He didn't break a leg or something so he couldn't come. He cheated, he—"

Martha Morse was almost frightened at his sudden rage. She interrupted quietly, "Hadn't you better open the box, Ronnie? Let's see what's in it."

"I don't *want* to open it. I don't care what's in it," he stormed. "I—"

"Well, I do," she said firmly. "A box marked 'Christmas' is always worth looking into. Of course, it has your name on it, but—"

"I don't care whose name is on it. Open it if you want to—I'm not the tiniest bit interested. I never want to see what's in it." He turned his back and stood kicking his boot against the stair rail.

Martha Morse knelt beside the chest and slipped the bolt. When she lifted the lid an exclamation of pleasure escaped from her. It was a strange collection of things that Byron Flagg had gathered together. She lifted them out and spread them around her on the floor. There was a little cask of West Indies red peppers, a rare treat to northern appetites. Another little cask held rich brown sugar; there were great bunches of big blue raisins wrapped in fine oiled silk; and in other silken packages Turkish paste and strange sweets from the East, dried fruits and nuts. There were tamarind preserves and preserved ginger in gray-blue jars and, at the very bottom, a lovely teakwood box.

Mrs. Morse held the box on her lap unopened and looked up at Ronnie's grim back. He was staring out of the tower window, silent now for want of breath.

"Wouldn't you like to open this box, Ronnie?" she asked gently. "It's not fair that I should have all the fun. Byron Flagg must have been collecting treats for us for months. Probably he traded with every passing ship that he could get to put off a boat."

"That's just it! That's why I'm so mad, Aunt Marthy." All Ronnie's anger flared up again. "He's a bad old man and I'd like — I'd like to swim straight to New Brunswick where he's gone. I'd like to burst open the door and tell him how I despise him. I'd — "

"*I'm* to open the box, then, am I, Ronnie?" Aunt Martha interrupted.

"I won't. Go ahead if you're so curious. He can't buy me," Ronnie said rudely.

Mrs. Morse lifted the cover of the teakwood box. On the top, with her name pinned to it, lay a lovely Cashmere shawl. Below were carved whalebone and ivory toys. Such things as sailors made to while away the weary hours on shipboard were no novelty to Martha Morse, but she had never seen more beautiful workmanship than these. There was a little whale boat complete in every last detail — its bow box and stern locker; its rowlocks and its six oars of varying lengths; the tiny tubs in their places, each with its coiled lines carved in minute perfection. There were the harpoons and lances, their sheathed tips resting in the cleats, the buckets, the

44

water keg — all the work of days and days. She could see homesick men on quiet seas, waiting for a breeze to fill their sails — big hands with cunning fingers fashioning in miniature the tools of their craft.

"How some boys would treasure these," she said. "This harpoon, now —"

But Ronnie was relentless. "I could harpoon that man my own self. He's just a selfish old man," he stormed.

"Maybe he *is* selfish," she agreed, "but I think he has parted with things he's treasured all his life long — just to make amends to us." Ronnie was not listening, and

45

she went on thinking out loud. "This shawl, for instance. Like as not he chose this cream with shades of violet himself. For some gold-haired girl with pansy eyes, no doubt. I wonder why he never gave it to her. And here's a letter with both our names on it."

"I don't want to read his old letter. I won't listen to it," Ronnie said.

Suddenly an idea came to him. He turned to his aunt in excitement. "Aunt Marthy! I know what! We can fire the cannon! Then somebody'll have to come and take us off the Rock. Why didn't we think of it before!"

Martha Morse looked at the boy in amazement. "Fire the cannon?" She spoke as if she could not possibly have heard correctly. "Why, Ronnie, that cannon is for emergencies!"

"Well, isn't this a — a 'mergency?" Ronnie wanted to know.

Mrs. Morse's patience was at an end. "No, it's not," she said firmly. "An emergency — the kind that cannon is for — means there's a ship off there on the Ledges, breaking up. There are helpless sailors — clinging like little black ants to spars — being washed off into Eternity while you watch. No, Ronnie, this is no emergency.

We are two able-bodied beings left to guard a light! And we'll do it — Christmas or not! And, what's more, we'll do it without all this self-pity, these tantrums."

Ronnie was startled out of his sense of grievance. "But, Aunt Marthy —" he began.

"I've heard enough, Ronnie," his aunt interrupted. "Nobody's going to spoil my Christmas. Not Byron Flagg, and not a sniveling small boy either."

"But I'm not sniveling!" Ronnie was indignant.

"You might as well be. You've gone all to pieces because you're missing a Christmas party at school and a measly stocking full of candy."

"That's not true. And you're just as disappointed as I am this minute."

"Of course I am. And with more reason too," Martha Morse told him. "You'll have fifty more Christmases in your life probably. But I won't. And the chance to lift my voice to the Lord in the old Christmas hymns, with my neighbors and friends around me in the peace of a Christmas service, is more precious than you can understand at your age. But Christmas, Ronnie, is something in your heart. It's a feeling that doesn't go with anger and hatred. And my heart's got to be clean and ready for Christmas. It's going to be as clean as this lighthouse, Ronnie. I can't even be angry with you, child."

Then she added more gently, "Go to your room now, Ronnie. I'll finish what has to be done. And I'll do it best alone—under the circumstances. I'm not punishing you. I know you're not the spoiled urchin you'd like me to believe. But I know you'll feel better when you've cooled off and had time to think. What you need at the moment is some real lonesomeness. Run along now, child, and get it."

All the rest of that day Ronnie sulked while his aunt scrubbed and polished and dusted in a kind of holiday ecstasy. He ate his meals in silence and she ignored him cheerfully.

Christmas Eve

ON THE day before Christmas Martha Morse cooked and baked. Good smells of spices and molasses and brown sugar crept through the lighthouse and up the winding stairs until the very walls seemed to sniff in pleasure. She was through at last and changed into her dark red merino with its braided yoke and sleeves.

The short afternoon drew to a close; the feeling of breathless expectancy that comes before every Christmas Eve began to exert itself. The comfortable, shining common room with its sparse dignity, the gray-walled tower with its soaring grace, quieted themselves to wait. Something was to be born anew into the world. This night the ageless Christmas miracle would repeat itself.

At sunset Martha Morse rapped on the door of Ronnie's bunk room. She carried Byron Flagg's letter in her apron pocket.

"Ronnie, it's time to light the lamp. Will you come? Or shall I go alone? I can manage if you'd rather not." Her voice was gentle but cheerful.

Ronnie opened his door and stepped out on the landing. He avoided looking at her. "I'll come, Aunt Marthy. I haven't been any help today," he added.

"Well, I've been too busy to notice," she told him briskly. "But just run down and see the tea table before we go aloft. I think it looks real nice."

Ronnie ran down the short flight of stairs. He gave a little gasp at sight of the table. It stood against the wall with their places set at either end, and its smooth pine surface was almost hidden with good things that Aunt Martha had somehow contrived. For a centerpiece a monumental brown cake, crusty and fragrant, bursting with raisins and nuts, formed a sort of bold headland at whose feet lay a white beach of tiny stones. And drawn up on the beach was the little carved whale boat with all the whaling gear spread out on shore for overhauling. There were cookies trimmed with bits

of candied fruit, sliced corned beef in a wreath of red stars cut from the West Indies peppers, tiny dishes of the rare preserves sparkling against the wholesome background of brown bread. And, from the back of the stove where they stood, came the fragrance of simmering potatoes.

Ronnie swallowed once or twice but no words came at first. Martha Morse, watching from the bottom step, could feel his pleasure and was completely satisfied.

"Gee, Aunt Marthy, it's—it's pretty," he got out finally. "And I'll bet you had the corned beef tonight because it's red—for Christmas. And you cut out all those little stars yourself!"

"I'm relieved to hear you call them stars," she said lightly. "I was afraid they'd look so much like starfish that they'd spoil your appetite."

"They're lovely stars, Aunt Marthy," Ronnie assured her. "I never once thought of starfish—at least not till you said it first." They laughed comfortably together as they started up the winding stairs.

The lamp chamber always gave Ronnie a strange feeling. You reached it breathless from the long climb, but at the top step something else took over. The sea piling up to the horizon, the expanse of sky, the bold swooping and circling of the gulls lifted you somehow. You felt light as air, as though you had only to lay a finger gently on a gull's claw to go off and up.

But tonight there was something more. The whole chamber was diffused with color, a dull green and gold from the glow still lingering in the western sky. It gave everything a gentle radiance of its own. Ronnie pressed his nose against the windowpane and looked out to sea. It was fairly quiet. There was no wind, no waves to speak of, but the whole sea seemed to rise and fall and heave with lazy power. And it too was as green and bronze in the strange light as molten metal. A few careless snowflakes drifted down; a few sleepy gulls made last dips and circles, and their mewing was hushed and came softly to him through the glass.

Ronnie felt as if some hard kernel within him had suddenly begun to swell, to expand. He looked quickly at Aunt Martha to see if she looked different. And she did. Her quiet face was so glowing in the fading light that he wanted to throw his arms around her and hold her close because she was too beautiful to bear.

"Aunt Marthy," he said in a small voice, "do you remember what you said yesterday about Christmas? Christmas in your heart, I mean?"

"Yes, I remember," she told him. "And you've got some of it tonight, haven't you?"

"Well, you told me to think, and I've done a lot of it since yesterday. And somehow this old Rock doesn't seem so bad tonight. It's—it's beautiful up here right now. And this queer light must be something special just for Christmas Eve."

His aunt nodded, but she did not speak.

"You know what, Aunt Marthy?" Ronnie went on after a pause. "I'd like to hear that Byron Flagg's letter after all, I guess."

"So would I, Ronnie, so I brought it up," she told him. "We'll light our lamp and then we'll read it."

Together they lighted the great wicks and adjusted them; together they swung the door shut and made fast the catch; together they set the carriage revolving. Then Aunt Martha gave a sigh of satisfaction and murmured softly under her breath her little evening prayer.

"A straight, true light. God help you to protect all souls at sea this night."

The flame pulled up, then settled to a steady glow. The mechanism steadied to its long night's course. Out across the darkening water it swung its message of assurance. They watched it for a moment, stirred as always to see what they had set in motion, but humble too. Then Martha Morse drew the boy down beside her to a step around the first bend, out of the flash and grinding noise. She pulled the keeper's letter from her apron pocket and read it aloud in the dim half-light.

Dear Mrs. Morse and Ronnie,

I have played you a mean trick. Yes, and I planned it long and careful. I don't expect to get much happiness out of it either. But let me tell you the reason. I am more than sixty years old and I have never yet spent a Christmas with a parcel of young ones. I was an only child, we lived a long way from any neighbors, I shipped to sea at ten, and so it went. Last Christmas I promised myself I would spend this one with my niece's family — there's seven of them, all told. And when I couldn't get relieved, I took this way. Please try to think kinder of me than I deserve.

Byron Flagg

There was a long pause when she had finished. Ronnie sat so still he might have been asleep.

"Well? Do we go on hating him?" she asked at last.

"Poor mean old man," Ronnie said finally. Then he laughed a little rueful laugh. "If he came pounding on the sea door right this minute — wanting his old light-house back for Christmas — I wouldn't want to give it to him. I guess, Aunt Marthy, I want to be right here tonight."

"I guess I do too," she told him softly.

They sat watching their bit of stair and tower wall lighten and darken as the lens swung round, and then

Ronnie went on slowly, "All over the world, on Christmas Eve, people are putting little candles in their windows, to light the Christ Child on His way. They're doing it right now, aren't they? This very minute! It's almost the very nicest of all the special things we do on Christmas."

He groped a little for the right words. The thought that had come to him would take good words.

"We've lighted a candle tonight too—a big one. We've lighted the biggest candle we'll ever have a chance to light for Him—to help Him on His way."

He leaned against her suddenly and he gave a long, long sigh of perfect content. Then he added softly, "Aunt Marthy, Tern Rock Light's the loveliest place in all the world to spend His birthday."

If, that Christmas Eve, over dark water, a small dark lad in eastern dress, with sandaled feet, happened to follow a flashing light to a distant lighthouse, He would find all in readiness within.